Flirting with Death

Kayla Frederick

This is a work of fiction. All the characters and events portrayed in this novel are either products of the author's imagination or are used fictitiously.

Flirting With Death

Story was previously published in "Flirting with Death: A Collection of Short Stories & Poems"

Cover by betibup33
Edited by Rita Delude
Library of Congress Control Number: 2023952120
ISBN: 9781950530250
First Edition 2023

1.

THE MUSIC WAS loud, each beat echoing through Claudia's skull as she stepped to the rhythm, shaking her hips in time to the beat. The crystals on her hip belt clanked together, the lights reflecting a hundred different colors as she swayed. Even though the aisle between tables was narrow, she had no fear about bumping into any of the people seated near her. Her steps were practiced, careful. The darkness helped her forget that there was a crowd as she moved between the tables. If the lights had been on to their full capacity, it would've been much harder to ignore the fact that there were at least a hundred pairs of eyes on her.

At last, the music came to an end, and Claudia was covered in sweat. She wondered how visible it was to the audience as she curtsied and bowed. Among a sea of applause, she slipped away to the back room. A few girls she passed patted her on the back, congratulating her on her performance. Their heavily made up faces twisted into expressions that resembled smiles but lacked the necessary happiness behind them. Not that she could blame them. She probably had a similar expression.

"Good show," Persima, one of the younger dancers called and extended a water bottle.

Claudia gulped down the water, twisting the cap back on before she said, "Thanks."

Persima offered her a smile so wide Claudia could see the lipstick on her teeth as she made her way to the floor. Claudia watched her go before she went over to the vanity, setting her mostly empty water bottle on the edge. When she did, she caught sight of her reflection and took a moment to study herself. Her Romani heritage showed in her light brown skin and wavy black hair. She had a thin face and narrow eyes. She was pretty in a non-traditional sort of way. Between the bra and sarong on her bedlah, her skin shone with sweat.

Claudia never thought she'd make her living by dressing like *that* for crowds, but she gave herself a proud smile just the same. She loved to dance; it was the only thing that made her feel complete. Hard to believe that only a few years prior, she'd been employed at the Houston Police Department.

How quickly life could change.

She embraced it though. She was a star in that place. It wasn't ideal, but they paid her well enough. It was better than the other option—working in a strip club. At least it was a family restaurant with all different types of entertainment, belly dancing just one of them.

Claudia tucked a strand of hair behind her ear and finished her water. Since she was still, she was beginning to cool down. She grabbed a towel to wipe away any remaining traces of sweat before she gathered her clothes from her locker. As soon as the leggings and loose sweater fell into place, she felt more like herself.

Hanging up her sweaty costume in a place where it would be washed before her next appearance, she made sure everything was in check. Slinging her small pleather bag over her shoulder, she left the building. The chilly evening air brought goosebumps to her damp skin despite the thickness of her sweater.

Just as she'd had the thought, her phone started to ring. She plucked it from the side pocket of her bag and sighed when she saw it was her mother calling. The home her parents offered her though was a safe haven. A place she could live while she worked on getting her life together once again. She was grateful.

Not everyone had parents who were so generous, parents who were so caring. Living with her parents wasn't as bad as other people her age pretended it was, but she'd be lying if she said she didn't miss her space. It seemed like the time she'd spent living on her own hadn't lasted nearly long enough.

"Hello, Momma," Claudia said.

"Dia, honey, it's past dark," her mother said. Though her voice was sweet and concerned, there was just a hint of a warning there too.

"I know, Momma," Claudia said. "One of the girls called in today so I covered some of her shift. I actually just clocked out, and I'm about to start my walk home."

"You should let your father come get you. It's too dangerous for you to be walking alone this time of night," her mother replied at once.

Claudia rolled her eyes. They had this same argument every time Claudia went to work, and her mother never won. She wasn't one to back down though. "No need," Claudia said and let out a light chuckle. "It's just a few blocks, I'll be fine. Just as I always am."

"It only takes one time, *dragă*," her mother insisted. "Why take the risk?"

Claudia was touched at her concern, but only slightly. A lot of it drew from what had already happened to Claudia, and that was the part that made her shrug off the concern. If she had stared danger in the face once and survived, she could do it again. She was confident of that much.

"I love you, Momma," Claudia said and hung up before her mother could protest.

Before the phone call, she'd been at ease, but then the night had a menacing edge. With a sigh, she tucked the phone away and steeled her shoulders, ready to begin the trip home. A lot of women were afraid to walk these streets at night, but Claudia wasn't. She was so used to the walkways, the alleys, that she was confident in her abilities to escape from danger. Even though she was a fairly attractive girl, she had gotten into the habit of dimming her appearance outside of work and walking in a way that hardly drew anyone's eye.

She did it on purpose. A ritual designed to barricade her work self from her true self. For as much as she wanted to believe she was the same person in both places, she wasn't. In everyday life, she wasn't confident or strong. She was just…*her,* the girl who risked danger on a daily basis because life without it was flavorless.

2.

FOR AS MUCH as León Noyer wanted to look like an average Joe on the Houston streets, he stood out. He was French, a fact that seeped itself into every facet of his identity. Not only did he have striking features that made him look not quite American, but he had a thick accent to boot. That fact still struck León as odd since he'd only lived in France until his tenth birthday.

Then he'd been kicked to this country that he still couldn't decide if he liked or hated. The food was good. That was the thought on his mind as he sat in the restaurant, picking sparsely at the remaining traces of his dinner. Even though he sat alone, he gathered no attention. That brought a smile to his face as he popped a bite of food into his mouth, savoring the taste.

He worked the best when he blended in, just another guy in the crowd. While the attention of the people in the restaurant had their eyes on the women dancing their way through the dining room, he had his eyes on them. The dinner patrons had no idea they were on display. He cased every woman at the three tables around him. Frowning, he set his fork down in a way that would make the least amount of noise possible.

While he was sure that he hadn't drawn anyone's eye, he had no way of knowing for sure. An attractive man sitting alone might have spurred talk among the waiters and waitresses.

León rolled his shoulders, moving his eyes from surrounding patrons to the dancers themselves. Most of them were wearing so much makeup that he inevitably sneered. They were like giant dolls, fake in every way. The woman in his mind had to be perfect—long hair, thin body, dark eyes. Attractive. There were a lot of girls meeting that description within six feet of him, but none of them were *it*. Whenever he found the perfect girl, a feeling would surge through his gut, forcing out everything else in a kind of tunnel vision. That hadn't happened yet.

Not that night.

It had only been a few months since the last girl, but to León, it felt as if an eternity had passed. He had an itch that needed to be scratched, and the longer he took to do it, the riskier it would become. His self-control was already starting to slip, and he feared that he would be too desperate to fulfill his urges to worry much about the fallout.

Focus, he told himself.

Leaning his elbow on the table, he perched his chin on his hand, eyes on the nearest dancers. Their exotic outfits clanked and shone in the low light. When he thought about it, almost all of these women fit the description of the one he was looking for body-wise. The real problem was that most of them wore veils, so he couldn't tell what their faces looked like.

The longer he sat there, the more his hope started to fade. None of these girls would do. While a specific part of him stirred at their movements, it didn't connect with the deeper, primal urges inside him. Ready to call it a night, León plucked his wallet from his pocket and counted out a hundred dollars to throw down on his plate. He didn't know if that was too much. It probably was, but he wasn't worried about it. As a bounty hunter, he never worried about money because it was in steady supply.

Quickly, he rose and crossed the room, sticking close to the wall as he did so. No one said anything to him as he slid out into the night. He climbed into his truck, sitting in the darkness of the cab for a full minute before he started the engine. León tried to decide if he should scope out another place or just go home and see if tomorrow could offer him better luck. He was tired, and he knew that would be a hinderance to his hunt if the perfect girl *did* happen to stumble into his path.

Tomorrow's a new day, he thought sarcastically and pulled out of the parking lot.

As he eased himself onto the road, he caught sight of one of the dancers standing outside the restaurant, phone held to her ear. She was dressed in baggy jogging clothes, face clear of the mask that had concealed her. In the shadows, he couldn't make out her features clearly, but what he could see brought something to his stomach. A familiar stirring. As if she'd heard the thought, she looked up. Soft moonlight caught the edge of her jaw in a perfect highlight, and León's breathing picked up.

That was the girl.

León did a lap around the block, plan forming. When he saw her again, she was shuffling into the shadows toward the end of the street. She walked with purpose, and he wondered if that purpose came from fear or the need to be somewhere. He pulled up beside her, slowly rolling the window down. Partially, he expected her to look up at him with contempt or fear. Her eyes were bright as she stared back at him, expressing neither.

"Need a ride?" he asked, making sure his voice came out as a husky purr. He wasn't afraid to use his looks for evil. In fact, he'd found that it made the hunt even more fun albeit slightly unfair to his prey.

Her eyes flashed, the brightness ebbing out, before she said, "Oh, no thank you. I'm almost home." She took a step backward, back onto the sidewalk and started to hurry down the street.

León hung back, putting his truck into park as he watched her. He glanced up and down the street, weighing his options. He could grab her. They were far enough from the restaurant that he was sure no cameras could see him, and there was no one in sight. Breathing in and out, he flexed his fingers around the steering wheel, ready to sink them into her skin.

It's too risky. Even though there didn't *seem* to be any witnesses, it was an open area. There was no telling *who* was watching. *You know where she works, you can come back,* he added, trying against himself to be careful, to be smart.

It didn't work.

3.

THE WOMAN WAS thin and wiry, but she could *fight*. More so than León's previous two victims at least. He crept like a shadow. She hadn't even noticed he was behind her until his arm snaked around her waist. At first, he brought her close, to breathe in her scent. The terrified girl tried to pull away, elbowing him in the gut. He smiled at the pain. She was a fighter. It made the chase even more satisfying.

Slipping a pair of silver handcuffs from his back pocket, he hooked them around one wrist. The girl struggled even more, mouth open for a scream. He pressed his hand tight over her lips. In the moment of distraction, he wrenched her other arm behind her and secured the handcuffs. Panting, he held her close to him, one arm hooked around the small of her back, and the other still in place over her mouth.

She stopped fighting, her big eyes, staring up at him through the darkness. He couldn't read the expression, but a surge of pride rippled through him just the same. Just like with a bounty, he pushed her to the waiting passenger seat of his truck, wrists secured behind her. Once she was seated, he reached over her to strap her in, the jasmine scent of her perfume filling his nose once more. There was a faint tinge of something just beneath it, sweat and fear.

A delicious combination. León hurried into the driver's seat and pressed hard on the gas, eager to get them away from the scene of the crime. As he drove, he expected something from her, screams or a struggle to get the handcuffs off, but she did neither. She sat there, staring out the dashboard before she blinked and directed her gaze to him. Even without looking in her direction, he could feel her stare burning a hole in the side of his face. There were no tears, no desperate pleas, nothing he'd come to expect from his hunts.

Just that cold, dead stare.

"I know who you are," she said in a soft voice so low he barely heard her.

Doubt it, he thought but risked a glance at her from the corner of his eye anyway.

"You're the Houston Butcher," she whispered in that indecipherable tone.

He made no reaction. The only other time he'd been called that was within the scope of an agonized scream. León kept his eyes on the road, expecting the hysteria to sink in since she knew the severity of her situation. When it didn't, he drew his eyebrows together and glanced at her again from the corner of his eye. He was shocked to see she was *smiling.*

"Why are you doing that?" he demanded, slamming his palm to the steering wheel. "Stop it."

The smile grew, and she tucked her bottom lip in her teeth. "I-I'm sorry. I guess I'm just sort of star struck."

León was confused, so caught off guard, that he couldn't hide the fact that he was. Fear he was used to. Sadness, begging, desperation, and even hopeful bargaining, sure, they were all something he'd encountered. That was not. *Was that the point? To confuse him so much he'd be too distracted to notice her working up a plan to escape?*

He chuckled darkly. It was a formidable idea, but he wouldn't let it work. He wasn't that foolish. "First time I've ever met a girl excited to die."

"Not *excited* to die so much as ready. I had a near death experience not that long ago, and well…I guess it doesn't really matter. Bottom line? I *love* serial killers. Oh, my God. Ted Bundy,

Jeffrey Dahmer, Richard Ramirez…I've studied them all. Never thought I'd actually die doing what I love! Studying killers."

León licked his lips. He wanted to laugh because surely, she must be joking, but he didn't. He tried to dissect that statement, to decide if that was how she actually felt. He'd heard of groupies for all kinds of things but had never imagined they could exist for someone like him.

There's a first time for everything, he thought.

He was sure this game would be over as soon as he got her inside his house. Things would get back to normal then, and not a moment too soon. Eagerly, he pulled the truck to a halt beside the curb outside his house. He turned to look at her through narrowed eyes, expecting some change in emotion. The smile was still there, and he was more certain that it was all a joke.

There was no way she was honestly excited for him to kill her. She tilted her head to catch his eye in a way that bared her throat to him. His eyes dropped to the creamy brown skin. Did she expect him to strangle her right in the car?

Blinking back the desire, he opened the door and climbed out of the truck, circling it to her door. He expected her to lock it, keep a barrier between the two of them, but the door opened with ease. She watched him, head still tilted. He almost expected her to have gotten the handcuffs off sometime during his bafflement and make a dash for it.

León reached into the seat, undoing her seatbelt. His hand grazed behind her back. The handcuffs were still in place, and he grabbed the chain, pulling it to hoist her out of the truck. She stumbled down the step, pressing against him as she tried to regain herself. He pushed her away enough to put distance between them but kept the hand on her arm. Regardless of what she claimed, he still didn't trust her to not make a last minute dash for freedom.

There were neighbors on either side of him, and León's shoulders were tense with the assumption that she would notice and would scream her lungs out. That she would fight, doing anything in her power to gain someone's attention. She did neither. She walked with her head high directly into the lion's den.

As soon as the door closed behind them, she glanced around the shadowy living room before turning toward him. That huge smile was painted on her face again. "Nice place you've got."

"How kind of you to notice," he said, carefully rolling up his sleeves to his elbows. What was about to come would be messy, and he'd hate to dirty his shirt. It was one of his favorites.

She leaned toward him and whispered, "Where to?"

León's skin prickled with gooseflesh, arousal flushing through him as he became aware of how close she was. He had never been so titillated with someone before. He had to remind himself this wasn't a date. He *was* in the middle of an abduction.

León scoffed, some of his urge dwindling away to curiosity and *rage*. Did her reaction have something to do with *him*? Was he not frightening? Did she really think that she was *safe* with him?

"What the hell?" he demanded at last, hands clenching into fists at his sides. "Why aren't you afraid?"

She recoiled and shrugged. "I don't know. I'm just…not. I guess I never imagined myself to live a long life. Growing old has always seemed depressing to me. You are a budding serial killer. Being taken out by you? I'll be immortalized right alongside you as one of your young victims. I'll never have to be old. Never have to worry about everything that comes with a long life. I'll just be…done."

León blinked. So grim. He was the murderer and yet *he* was freaked out. He no longer thought she was joking about her feelings. This was a dead woman walking.

"I just wish my MP3 player was charged," she continued on. "I have the *perfect* playlist for something like this. If you don't mind me borrowing yours, I'd love to point you in the direction of a couple songs you might like."

León reached up, tapping his fingers to his temple. "I don't have an MP3, and what the fuck if I did? You're really not even gonna *try* to fight me? *Try* to escape?" He held his hands out to either side of him, pulling her attention to the airy expanse of his house. If she wanted to, she could make a good run for it.

Her bottom lip jutted out in a semi-pout, and she shook her head, scattering her dark waves. The dim light of his living room gave him the clearest picture of her yet. She was prettier than he'd guessed. Why was a girl like her so *morbid*?

"No, I'm not," she said and looked around. "Unless you want me to, of course. Totally up to you." A pause. "Hey so from what the police said, you have like a torture room full of all kinds of knives and stuff. Is that true or were they just guessing?"

León wanted to snap out something witty and clever, something to disarm that twinkling light in her eyes, but he was out of words. Had something this bizarre ever happened to a serial killer before? He doubted it.

The woman's shoulders slumped as she watched his expression. "Oh no. I came on too strong, didn't I?" she asked. "I'm sorry it's just…come *on*. How often am I going to get this chance, right? Just this once, hopefully." Then she laughed. Actually *laughed*.

"You're really not scared," León said, but it wasn't a question. Just a statement of the facts like she had done while assessing him in the truck. Now that he was beyond angry, beyond confused, he wanted to understand. "You…you *accept* me? *Accept* what I am?"

The woman sat down on his nearby armchair, hands still bound in the handcuffs. "Yeah, why wouldn't I?"

"I'm about to *kill* you," he said and wished he could speak her native language. If he could, maybe he could get the message across better.

She shrugged. "From what I understand, serial killers kill because something in them is hurting. Some part craves love that they either never got as a kid or think they're never going to get because of some inadequacy. I…it's sad actually. If all the world's killers had had different upbringings, happy ones, they might have never killed at all. Definitely food for thought."

León wrinkled his nose but didn't approach her. "How do you know all this?"

"I used to work forensics a couple years back," she said. "There was an incident, and I had to resign. Now, I'm trying to be a thriller author. I like to write about serial killers. They…fascinate me."

"That's a quirk," he said, eyebrows lifted in genuine fascination. He was impressed.

She bobbed her head and looked around. "Right? So…I'd hate to throw off your plans more than I probably already have. Let's get down to business."

León stroked the pocket with his knife and approached her slowly. She didn't flinch away as he reached for her. Her dark eyes stared up at him, ready for the death she thought was coming. That was the moment he made up his mind. When his fingers dipped into his pocket, he felt the cold blade of his knife but reached for the tiny key beside it instead.

4.

LEON WASN'T QUITE sure what it was that led him to undo her handcuffs, but the thought of massacring her no longer held appeal. As soon as the handcuffs dropped off, he expected her to swing at him, to jump up, and say it was all a lie. She stayed in the chair, rubbing her sore wrists and looking up at him through wide, hopeful eyes.

"What's next?" she asked again.

He didn't think as he reached down and took her hand, helping her to her feet. She walked beside him with ease as if she'd known him a long time. As if she knew *anything* about him. When she realized he was leading her to the front door, she stopped, needling him with questions.

"Where are we going?

Aren't you going to follow through?

Did I do something wrong?"

For as much as he wanted to be annoyed, he wasn't. He watched her with amusement, the way normal people watched puppies. He dared to say he was *joyful*. For the first time in his life, it was as if someone could see him.

All of him.

She allowed him to buckle her into the passenger seat of the truck, but when he climbed into the driver seat, she frowned.

"Where are we going?" she asked.

"I'm taking you home," he replied. "Where do you live?"

She didn't speak at first, the bafflement he'd worn twenty minutes prior then on her face. He stared back until she hesitantly began to give him directions for a place a few streets over. The drive was silent. When he pulled up in front of the house that she claimed to live in, her shoulders slumped. He hardly noticed as he studied the house. It was nice. Easily larger than his, and he doubted it was *really* her home. *What kind of person gives their address to a serial killer after all?* After everything she had said though, he couldn't escape the doubt that it might actually *be* her house.

That only made him more curious about her.

Her huge eyes focused on him as he waited for her to climb out.

"You're really letting me go?" she asked, sounding disappointed.

León clenched onto the steering wheel, forcing himself to not look at her. He still hadn't made up his mind that this was really a good idea. She knew his face, she knew where he *lived,* but he didn't want to have it any other way. Softly, she repeated her question, but he stayed frosty. The door opened and shut. He turned his head enough to watch her walk up the path. She opened the front door, light spilling out to illuminate her figure as she cast him a longing glance before the door rattled shut behind her.

León didn't move at first, a crushing wave of sadness consuming him at the thought of never seeing her again. Shaking his head to clear it, he eased his truck out of park and went about his way. A drive was just what he needed to take his mind off things. He tried to process it all, but the more he thought, the less sure he even was that all of it had happened. Just to prove a point to himself, he drove past her house again.

Like a bolt from the blue, the reality of what he'd done leaked in. He had let her go. He had let a *victim* go.

Palms sweating, León decided to drive home. His work had provided him with a few friends at the station. If she tried to file a report, they'd give him the benefit of the doubt. He'd use that to say he was questioning her in relation to a bounty. It wasn't great, but he was sure his friends would believe him, and their certainty would be enough to convince whoever else needed to hear it.

In the meantime, all he could do was go home and wait to see what would happen next.

5.

CLAUDIA GOT ONE last glimpse of the man in the truck. Even though it was dark, she was confident he was watching her too. As she closed the door, she wondered what he had been thinking. Wondered why he had decided to let her go to begin with.

I don't have friends. I can't keep a job. And apparently, I'm serial killer repellent, she thought.

Before her disappointment could overwhelm her, she was ambushed with a hug from her mother. She was a stout woman, her tuft of brown hair going up Claudia's nose as she squeezed her daughter tight.

"I thought something bad happened to you, *dragă.* I was worried."

Claudia laughed, trying to smile even though her lips wanted to do anything but. "I'm fine, Momma, really. I just caught up with an old friend."

"If you insist," the woman said, pulling away.

"I do," she said.

"Okay, well, dinner is in the fridge if you get hungry."

"Thank you, Momma," Claudia said and kissed her mother on the top of the head before she passed her.

Food was the last thing on her mind. As she trudged to her room, all she could think about was the strange man. The Houston Butcher. She closed her door with a click, locking it for added effect. She still couldn't decide exactly what had happened, why she was still alive. Whatever she had said had changed his mind.

I talked too much, she scolded herself. *Even still, he would make an excellent character.*

She plunked down in the seat in front of her desk and opened her laptop. She was ready to write everything that had happened but stopped, staring at the blinking cursor. Her thoughts were impossible to summon in a line or two. After all, what did it mean to be *rejected* by a serial killer? He'd liked her enough to abduct her, but something had changed between the time he put her in the truck and the time they'd gotten back to his house. It was so unbelievable that she tried to find a way to incorporate it into her story but could not.

For everything she knew, serial killers didn't let their victims go. Once they had someone picked out and a plan of action in mind, they hardly derailed from it. Except he had. He had let her go knowing that if she wanted to, she could go straight to the police. She could get him arrested.

He had risked it just the same.

I spooked him, she thought in silent awe. Then again with different emphasis. I *spooked* him.

6.

L EON WENT THROUGH the next day with bated breath. He was sure that at any moment, his cop buddies would call or stop by with the woman's testimony, and he'd be at risk for everything to come out. As the sun rose and began to sink once again, nothing happened. He sat in his front room, in the armchair she'd rested in, and considered the possibility that she *hadn't* gone to the police.

She really wanted me to kill her, León thought, unsure how to process that.

It was good news for him, of course, but it did little to satiate that urge. Sure things were clear, but his itch still needed to be scratched. He'd been so eager to feed it last night but had only managed to tease himself. Then the urge was coming back with a vengeance. Confusion aside, he needed a successful hunt. León could hardly wait for it to be dark before he was in his truck, scoping out the women in a few nearby clubs. Strip clubs were definitely *not* his favorite place to be, but they made it easy to canvass. His search offered him several potential candidates, but none of them stuck with him the way the woman from the previous night had.

Frustrated, he retreated back to his truck and sat in the dark seat, chewing on his lip. Women had thrown themselves at him all night, but all he could think of was the one who had gotten away. Or rather the one he'd *let* get away. He hadn't even bothered to get her name.

Why does it matter? he chastised himself.

Knowing more details about her than what she'd revealed would do nothing to help him. Somehow, he shook himself out of it and eased the truck down the road. It wasn't long before the perfect woman came into view. She was tiny, smaller than the woman the day before even, and she was walking alone. Her arms were folded across her chest, and every few steps, she paused to glance over her shoulder. He could hardly see her face, but León was at the point where it didn't matter.

He needed a kill. It would be a case of wrong place at the wrong time for her.

As if she'd heard the thought, she started to move faster. There was a woman not ready to accept her own demise. Smiling, León circled the block slowly, trying to get his supplies together in the passenger seat to make the grab. When he saw the woman again, she hurried across the street, her long black hair reflecting bits of the streetlight overhead.

León stopped. The hair made him think of the mystery woman again. Frowning, he tried to push the experience away, to focus on the situation at hand. The woman vanished into a stretch of shadows up ahead, and even though she was in prime position, León found he'd lost the drive to pursue her.

"Damn it," he said out loud, slamming his palm to the steering wheel.

Maybe he would find out mystery woman's name after all.

7.

WHEN CLAUDIA WOKE up the next day, she didn't let herself think about what had happened the night before. It'd do her no good to dwell on it though the man's beautiful face had haunted her dreams. At work, she threw herself into her dancing, glad for the stress relief. She danced until she was so exhausted she feared she might actually collapse and looked forward to getting a good night's sleep.

The music changed tempo, and she stepped in tune, throwing her arms out. Under the lights her skin seemed to shimmer. With the faintest hint of a smile, she looked into the shadowy crowd, purposefully not looking at any one person. She could've sworn she caught a glimpse of the Butcher. Just as soon as she saw him, the image disappeared, and she was sure it was all in her head.

He'd let her go. Why would he come back?

When the end of her dance came, she wasn't ready to leave. She wanted to stay until she was so tired, she'd have a hard time keeping her eyes open. She pleaded with a few other girls to swap with her but none of them agreed. Resigned, she went through the process of changing her clothes and cleaning herself up.

It looked as if she'd have another long night before her. Slinging her bag over her shoulder, she called home to let her mom know she was on her way. Just like the night before, she started the trek home. Head down, she walked onward though every few steps she couldn't help but glance over her shoulder, hoping to see a familiar truck.

The street was empty, and she was mad at herself for being like that, for being *disappointed* that the Butcher wasn't out there waiting for her. What kind of person was she to be so excited by the thought of her own death? Sighing, she tucked her hands into her pockets. She had never been okay. That was the *real* reason her parents let her stay with them, she knew. They were scared of what she might do to herself if she were left unattended for too long.

Apparently their fears were legitimate. She was a destructive force. Even coming to that realization didn't stop her from looking over her shoulder every time she heard an approaching car. Her hope would rise and fall in time to each flash of light from the headlights moving past.

He's not coming back, she told herself.

When she was two doors down from her parents' house, she heard the sound she'd been waiting for—the Houston Butcher's truck.

Claudia paused at once, looking up into the man's eyes as the truck came to a halt beside her. The window rolled down and familiar gray eyes peered at her.

"I could use a friend," he said.

8.

THE WOMAN'S EXPRESSION was so hopeful, that León almost changed his mind on the spot. He wasn't used to people being *happy* to see him, and he wasn't sure what to do with it. It seemed as if his entire life had been a series of scandals with him always in the middle of it. A troublemaker. He was a troublemaker, and that never inspired smiles. All it earned him were a steady series of frowns and scowls.

His behavior was what had forced his family to move to America to begin with. It was also the deciding factor that his father used to throw him out on his ass the second he turned eighteen.

So when the mystery woman's eyes lit up, he thought it had to be a prank. There was no way she'd thought of him in the same compacity he had of her. It'd be like a zebra being excited by a lion's attention. He held his breath, waiting to see what she'd do next. The woman didn't sense any of his doubts and fears. She nearly *skipped* to the truck and climbed into the passenger seat, giving him a full smile.

"It's good to see you again," she said, neatly buckling herself in as if they were old friends rather than killer and potential victim.

"It…is," León said uncertainly. He was surprised he meant it.

The uneasiness sat like a ball in his stomach as he pulled away from the curb, unsure of his own feelings. As he punched the gas and his truck went to the speed limit, he started to relax. The woman was silent, half a smile still lingering on her lips as she looked out the window. He glanced at her from the corner of his eye, curiosity eating away at him once again.

He wanted to wait until they were in the safety of his home, but the need to know won out. "Why didn't you go to the police?" he asked as they rounded onto his street.

"Huh?"

"You. You had all day to rat me out, but you didn't," he said, trying to keep his tone calm and even. He didn't want her to have any sense of how screwed up the thought had made him. "Why didn't you?"

She squinted, face scrunching up as if he had just asked her what the meaning of life was. At last she shrugged and said, "I didn't…want to?"

León licked his lips and tapped his palm to the edge of the steering wheel. "Walk me through your thought process. I don't understand."

The woman tilted her head from side to side. "There's nothing to understand really. I mean you picked me up and let me go. As a storyteller, I can tell you that makes for a terrible book."

"Yeah, but you know who and what I am. Don't you have some kind of moral compass? How can you not want to tell?"

She drummed her fingers on the light gray fabric of her jogging pants. "It wasn't my decision to make. Who am I to say you should go to jail? For all I know, you were just kidding about being the Houston Butcher. I mean, you didn't hurt me. Scared me a little bit, but you let me go home at the end of it without even a bruise. What's to be done?"

"Hmm," León said, considering. "Okay, let me play a quick game of hypotheticals with you. Say I took you to my red room. That I tortured you, roughed you up, and *then* let you go home. Would you have called the police then?"

"No," she said quickly.

León cut his eyes to her.

"I mean, *I* wouldn't have, but I couldn't guarantee the same for my parents. If they saw me in that condition, they would flip out. They already think I can't take care of myself, and well, that would be all the proof they'd need."

León thought about that as he pulled his truck into his driveway. "So you wouldn't have been concerned for your wellbeing? Worried that I would come back and finish the job?"

The woman frowned. "No. I was fine with the idea of you taking me out, remember?" A pause. "Is this why you came back to see me? You changed your mind?"

"Not exactly," he admitted, hating how hopeful she sounded. Instantly, she deflated, but he continued, "I have a bit of a problem."

"What's that?" she asked, leaning subtly closer to him. The angle gave León a fresh whiff of her scent.

"You said you worked forensics, that you've studied killers, right?"

"Right."

"I want your insight."

She sat up, tucking a thick tuft of her dark hair behind her ear.

"Sure," she said and clapped her hands together as if they were about to work on a project. "What is it?"

He turned to face her, giving his full attention as he said, "I tried to find another victim today."

It was impossible to miss the one eighty shift in her mood, and he felt bad. "Oh?" she asked, tone belying her face.

"Yeah," he said, shifting his gaze to the window beside her. "I had one all picked out. It would've been perfect. A stop and grab like I'd done with you but…"

She raised her eyebrows and said, "But?"

"I couldn't go through with it," he said, and his shoulders sagged. Admitting it out loud made him feel like a failure, and he hated it. Hated that he had decided to let those words out into the air where another human could hear them.

Her mouth opened into a little *O*, and she leaned toward him again, forcing him to focus on her rather than anything else. "Has that ever happened to you before?"

León regarded her, trying to decide what emotion she was wearing then. *Concern. Not mocking, not disgusted.* She didn't *look* at him as if he were a failure. "No," he said.

"Did I freak you out last night?" she asked. "Is that it? Because if I did…"

"She reminded me of you," he said, looking away as he cut her off. Again, he felt weak for admitting such a human thing. *This was a mistake*, he thought. Not for the first time.

The mystery woman clapped her hands together, pulling León's full attention once again. "That's your problem," she said excitedly.

He quirked his lip to the side. Of course it was a problem, but not in the way she probably thought. "Explain," he said, resting his forearms on the steering wheel. He was already exhausted, and the longer the conversation went on, the more energy he lost. The entire incident with the woman in the street seemed like ages ago, and he was ready to forget it.

"Well, in all my weirdness last night, I somehow went from a victim to…well, not. It was like you saw something in me, something that reminded you of the fact that I'm not just an object. When you saw someone who reminded you of me, the same kind of thing happened."

León drew his eyebrows together. It made a vague amount of sense. "Okay, and that matters how?"

"Well, if I'm not mistaken, serial killers see their victim as an object, a plaything for their amusement, right? They don't actually see the person themselves."

León had never put any thought into it before, but she was right. The woman had been a means to an end. He'd never been sorry for what he'd done, and he didn't regret it either. He hadn't even thought about the two girls he'd murdered after disposing of their corpses like they were bags of trash. Even the woman in his truck hadn't registered as anything more than a toy before she'd thrown him for a loop and knocked the predator right out of him.

"How can I see you as anything? I don't even know your name," he grumbled. "I did everything according to routine, and yet, something changed."

"Do you really want to know my name?" she asked.

"If your theory is correct, it won't make a difference, right? You've already cracked my armor, so we might as well be acquaintances. I suppose," he turned away, stepping out of the truck before she could see his face. The last thing he wanted was for her to see how vulnerable this conversation made him feel.

The woman was a moment behind him. He was glad for the shadows in front of his house. It made it easier to face her knowing she couldn't see whatever expression flitted across his face. She approached him with ease, nearly bouncing once again as she stuck her hand out and said, "My name is Claudia. Glad to make your acquaintance though I liked the friend title you mentioned earlier."

León returned the gesture. Her skin was smooth and soft, her grip delicate. "I'm León." He expected her to retract her hand once the greeting was over, but she held it tight. Her other hand reached up, and she stroked his fingers, eyes wide.

"What is it?" he asked, pulling his hand free with more force than he'd wanted to use. He told himself to stop being freaked out by the woman who was easily a foot and a half shorter than him and eighty pounds lighter, but she was a mystery.

"I'm sorry. It's just your hands are so big, so capable. You are an apex predator, and I think it's glorious," she said. He couldn't see her face, but somehow, he knew she was smiling just the same.

León felt his heartrate accelerate, and a warmth spread to his cheeks. *Was that a blush? Was he actually* blushing? *What spell has she cast over me?* He tried to hide it by saying, "Come on. Let's get inside before the neighbors see you."

"Yeah, yeah," she said, leading the way up the walkway and to his porch.

She stood to the side as he unlocked the door, ushering her inside. Once the door closed behind him, she turned to look at him through shining eyes. He pushed past her to the nearest table, turning the lamp on with a twist of his fingers.

Light flooded the room, and Claudia stood in her place by the door, looking around. León plopped into his armchair watching her.

"So what's next?" she asked.

He stared at her. He had no idea. He'd been so wrapped up in the idea of seeing her again, that he hadn't stopped to ask himself *why* he wanted to see her again. Now that she was there, what could they do? He had no idea. He'd never had many friends growing up, so he had no idea what it was that normal people did together.

Claudia smiled, picking up on the hesitation. "It's okay. You don't have to answer."

He gave her a small complimentary smile. It was genuine.

With a flourish of his wrist, he gestured to the sofa across from him. "Take a seat."

She bobbed her head and obeyed, sitting with her hands on her knees as she waited for him to speak again.

So obedient, he thought, and something in him was pleased with the thought. "So really though. What's your deal? On the outside, you're so pretty, yet on the inside you obsess over serial killers and write books about murder?"

Claudia tucked a strand of dark hair behind her ear and chuckled softly. "Oh, come now, León. You're not a serial killer yet. Need three victims for that title. That's why you need me. I am your crowning kill. Or I should be."

León assessed her. It seemed as if she were just as uncertain as he was…even for her show. Her hands were clasped together tightly between her knees, and even though she looked happy enough, there was the slightest hint of uneasiness about her.

"Yeah. No. Not gonna happen," he said, wagging a finger at her. "Nice try, but answer the question."

Claudia sighed, and the smile fell. She relaxed against the back of the couch, and her entire demeanor changed. It was as if she had just stepped out of a suit. "Growing up, I was always the outsider. The ugly duckling. The one person people never wanted to associate with. After I graduated high school, I had a fascination with forensics. I went to school and got a job with the Houston PD. I had access to serial killers that the public doesn't have. I talked to them sometimes, and the more I did, the more I realized that really my life wasn't much different from theirs. Somehow, I guess I got to thinking that either I would end up a killer or a victim because I can see it from both sides. I don't…understand the normal human brain."

León sat forward in his seat. Looking at her then, he would never have guessed any of that. In a strange sort of way though, he supposed it made sense. "Yeah, you mentioned the forensics thing. What happened with that? How do you go from police work to a belly dancer?"

"I told you I was let go."

"Yeah, but you didn't tell me *why*."

She swallowed and stared down at the floor.

"You wanted to be my friend," he encouraged. "This is how you do that."

She peered up at him through her lashes, conflicting expression as if she suddenly wasn't so sure of her own wishes. "We had a suspected killer in custody. I needed to do a cheek swab. You know for DNA. They sent me in the little interrogation room alone, and, well, no one knew that he had somehow undone his handcuffs. He took advantage of the situation, and things escalated. I was a hostage for a few hours until the police…"

"Shot him dead?" León finished. "Yeah, my buddies told me about that. I work as a bounty hunter, and they told me it as a cautionary tale. Never underestimate your opponent and all that."

"Yeah, well, the aftermath is what really sealed my fate. I wasn't deemed psychologically fit to return after that. I had a lot of unresolved feelings, and my parents started taking me to a therapist. He helped me try to turn my life around. I did what I could to change the way people saw me. I always thought belly dancers were beautiful, so I put my life into dancing. It wasn't as if I could use my degree anymore. Every police station around here has heard of the incident, and it'll follow me for the rest of my life." She looked downright sad then. It was the first time León had seen her as anything less than joyous to be in his presence. He didn't like it.

"And the books?" he asked, doing his best to keep the conversation going; although, her face and posture made it perfectly clear she wanted to do anything but.

"My therapist suggested I write my thoughts down to try to get a real grasp on my feelings. That turned to stories somehow."

León puffed his cheeks. "I suppose I can…understand that." He stared at her again, hardly blinking. Even with her backstory coming from her lips, it was still hard for him to picture her actually going through all of that.

He was so deep in his thoughts that he barely heard her say, "Your turn."

He blinked and came back to focus. She was watching him in a way that made his skin crawl. "No. I'm good."

She smiled at him, warm and encouraging. "Come on. You've already showed me the worst of you, and I accepted it. What are you afraid of?"

León was afraid of a lot of things, if he was telling the truth. He took in a deep breath, wondering where to begin. *If I haven't scared her off yet, this will do the trick,* he thought and began to speak. "I grew up in France. My father was a real bastard of a man. Beat me and my mother. Eventually, he killed her and somehow passed it off as suicide. People believed him, but I never did. I don't even remember how young I was when it happened, but even back then, I knew something was wrong. After that, it was just me and him for maybe a year."

He paused to wipe some of the moisture from his lips. Claudia bent forward, elbows on her knees as she hung onto his every word.

"Then Dad met another woman. I don't remember her name. What I do remember is her daughter. Delphine. Perfect little Delphy." In his head, he could still see her. A tiny thing with golden hair. A living doll. "I hated her from the first moment I saw her. She was always so happy and bright as if the world were a place that deserved such sentiment."

"What happened to her?" Claudia asked, voice thick and strained as if she already knew but didn't want to spoil it.

"I tolerated her at first, I really did," León said, reaching up to run his hand through his dark shaggy hair. "But I couldn't get over what my father had done. Hated the idea of him living happily ever after with this woman who had taken my mother's place."

Claudia blinked but said nothing.

"I used to hide out in the woods whenever I was having a particularly bad day. Well, one day, I lured her out there. So deep that I knew she wouldn't be able to go back home on her own. She came easily enough, didn't fight or anything. I think she was just so relieved that her *big brother* was finally showing interest in her." León chuckled, still able to see the little hopeful sparkle in her eyes. "If only she knew."

Claudia swallowed and wrapped her arms around herself, shifting subtly in her seat. The look she gave him then was the one he'd expected when they first met. The one that spoke of the monster inside him. It seemed out of place somehow.

"That part of the woods had a creek with a cliff over it. It wasn't a steep drop, but if you weren't careful, you could slip and bust your head on the rocks. Long story short, she walked up there, and I pushed her. She didn't die right away though. She hit her head and went unconscious. Dad had apparently been looking for us for a while because he found us out there."

"He suspected what I had done, but there was no proof either way. Delphine went into a coma. They did what they could to save her, but it didn't work. She'd lost a lot of blood, a lot of oxygen, and they suspected she'd be brain damaged if she ever woke up."

Claudia blinked. "Did she? Wake up?"

León shook his head. "In the end, they took her off life support. I don't remember how old she was."

"How old were you?"

"I was ten," León said. The memory of his tenth birthday being ignored in light of Delphine's situation still stung.

"Did you get in trouble for it?" Claudia asked.

"No. Dad was the only one who knew what I was capable of. Turned out a lot of people thought *he* was the one responsible. He became a social pariah. People started throwing rocks and stuff at our house. It got dangerous. Delphine's mother divorced my dad, and that was really all we had to stay in France for. That's why we came here. Fresh start and all that. Or not. The beatings got worse, and when I turned eighteen, Dad threw me out."

"That's awful. I'm sorry," Claudia said.

"Don't be. Best thing that ever happened to me really." León paused and gauged Claudia's face. Her eyes were wide, face contorted in suspense as she waited for his next words. There was no fear. Not even a trace of it. "Even after all that, you're still not afraid of me?"

She shook her head. "No."

"Huh," he said and clicked his tongue. "I think this might be the start of something beautiful."

9.

LEON WAS RIGHT. Days turned into weeks; weeks turned into a month. Claudia found herself in a new routine. One that largely depended on León. She would spend the day with her parents, her evening at work, and most nights at León's. The more time they spent together, the more she looked forward to it. For as oddly as their relationship had begun, things had taken a surprisingly normal turn.

Most days they watched movies or murder documentaries, laughing and eating popcorn. She was comfortable with him. Claudia had had dozens of friends who flitted in and out of her life during her college years, but none that felt as real as León.

As far as she could tell, he enjoyed her company as well, and that left her feeling elated. The only thing that hadn't changed was his desire to find a new victim though his efforts slowed considerably. With them spending so much time together, he'd had less to dedicate to his hobby.

Claudia was torn on how she felt about that. She was glad that no one else had died at his hands of course, but partly, she still wished he'd change his mind and make her his next kill. She brought it up once again about three weeks into their friendship, and he'd declined, still adamant that it would never happen. That only led Claudia to wonder exactly what he thought and felt about her. Did he only think about her as a friend or did his feelings go deeper? Was he even capable of feeling anything like that?

Claudia was too afraid of the answers to ask. So she went with it. Whenever León showed up at her job to pick her up, she went willingly to his house, never questioning what would happen.

When she got off work that night, there was no sign of him. She waited for a little bit, hoping he would appear, but he didn't. That wasn't too strange either, though. When her mother started to blow up her phone, she was forced to admit defeat and go home.

As soon as she walked through the door, her mother was waiting to pounce on her. "You're here tonight, young lady?" she asked, arms folded as she studied her.

Claudia nodded uncertainly and set her bag down in the usual place beside the door. She wasn't used to hearing her mother angry, and found she didn't like it. Though she couldn't say she blamed her. "Yeah. I'm probably going to get a snack and go to bed if that's alright."

"Of course, *dragă*, but I worry about you. I don't see much of you anymore. Where do you go when you're not home? Have you got your own place?"

"Work keeps me busy, Momma," Claudia said and ducked around her mother to go into the kitchen. The last thing she wanted was to tell her mother about León.

"You're a grown woman. Why do you still feel the need to lie to me?"

Her voice made Claudia freeze in place. She clutched the wall dividing the living room from the kitchen but didn't turn to look as she said, "I'm not lying."

"Then you'll tell me what his name is."

Slowly, Claudia turned back toward her mother. She had a scowl on her face, eyebrows raised in expected anticipation. If there was one thing she didn't approve of, it was men in her daughter's life.

Claudia knew that face, just as she knew better than to lie. "His name is León."

"Oh, and what does this *León* do for a living?" she demanded.

"Does it matter, Momma? He's just a friend," Claudia insisted, unsure if that was the truth or not.

"Hmm, just a friend, you say?" she tilted her head, clearly not believing her daughter's words. "A friend you spend the night with?"

"It's not like that."

"Then what *is* it like? Please tell me you're not letting him take advantage of you."

"Momma, I promise he's just a friend."

"If that's the truth then you'd talk to me about him, Dia."

Claudia closed her eyes. It was true. She used to chatter like a chipmunk about her friends and their exploits. "He's a bounty hunter."

"For the Houston P.D.?" her mother quipped, voice going shrill at once.

Hesitantly, Claudia bobbed her head and cracked open an eye to peer at her.

"You don't need to be hanging around him, *dragă*. He's no good."

Claudia held her hands out, knowing that her mother was only anchoring herself deeper into her memories, her fears about what her daughter had already been through. "He wasn't there when—"

"Doesn't matter. You don't need that kind of reminder. You've worked so hard to get better. Why would you throw all of that away now?"

"I'm fine, Momma," Claudia insisted. "I'm not throwing anything away. León is a good friend. All we do is watch movies and stuff. He makes me laugh. Besides, you're always saying I need more friends."

"I didn't mean men," she pointed out. "Men bring

nothing but trouble."

"If he's just a friend, what difference does his gender make?"

"How long have you known this boy? Staying at his house? I'm worried about his intentions."

Claudia laughed, thinking of the dangerous situation they had met under. If he hadn't been willing to hurt her then, he would definitely do nothing of the sort now. "I'm not."

"You may be an adult, but you agreed to follow our rules if you were to live under our roof. Honesty is important, *dragă*. I just want to help you."

Claudia's upper lip twitched. She loved her mother and father, but ever since the incident, she'd been suffocating in their love. There was no way to admit that without it sounding mean, coldhearted.

"I'll move out then," she said, with little to no emotion, and went to her room, idea of a snack abandoned.

"Claudia!" her mother bellowed behind her.

She slammed the door to her room, decision already made.

10.

LEON ROUNDED THE block toward the restaurant where Claudia worked. He had no plans of going inside, not that day. It was his attempt to keep some space between the two of them though he made a point to drive past her job as a way of feeling close to her. He liked having a friend who knew who and what he was. A friend who still accepted him, regardless of that information. At the same time, the vulnerability scared him. He wasn't used to feeling such human things, and that made him only want to cling tighter to her. Her friendship had been so wonderful so far that he feared he would do something stupid at any time and ruin it forever.

Sighing, he drove past the restaurant, slowing subtly as he did so. How badly he wanted to go inside, but he had to remind himself that some distance was good. For her and for him. Then he saw a shadow in the distance, the long wavy hair familiar. As he approached, the streetlights gave him more details. It was Claudia, and she was walking down the road with a bag slung over her shoulders, a suitcase dragging behind her.

León slowed beside her, trying to make sense of what he was seeing. "Hey, stranger."

She started and turned to look at him. There were dark circles under her eyes as if she'd been crying. "Hi, León. I thought I wouldn't see you today."

León leaned over the passenger seat and popped open the door, all reservations from earlier gone. "Get in."

Claudia obeyed, tossing her bags into the back before she climbed into the passenger seat. As León drove them toward his home he asked, "So what's going on?"

Claudia sighed and tucked a strand of hair behind her ear.

"I got into a fight with my mom and moved out. It's…been a long time coming."

"Sounds…serious," León said, having absolutely no idea how to sympathize with her. "What was the fight about?"

"My parents don't really want me to ever leave their sight. Mom wasn't so happy about how much time we've been spending together."

"You told her?" he asked, surprised.

Claudia bobbed her head. "Not so much as my absences haven't gone unnoticed."

León laughed. "Well, there's some irony. You got a place to go?"

Claudia hesitated, tucking her lip in and out of her teeth as if she were considering how to answer. "Not really. I kind of acted on impulse. I have some money saved, so I can probably make it in a hotel for a few weeks while I vet out an apartment."

"Fuck that. You can stay with me," he said, reaching over the middle console to set his hand on her knee. Even through her clothes, her skin was warm, and he wanted to keep his hand there.

"I couldn't ask something like that of you. I mean, we've just met," she said, eyes wide as she looked down at it.

León shrugged. "So what? It's only right since this is all probably my fault."

Claudia smiled then sighed, relaxing slightly in her seat. "Thank you, but honestly, it's no one's fault but my own. I've let my parents coddle me so much that they don't know what else to do."

León pulled the truck to a halt and climbed out. He pulled her bags out of the back, slinging one over his shoulder as he situated the other on the pavement. He led the way inside, Claudia closing the door behind him. They had gotten into the habit of settling into the living room whenever she was over, and that's where she stood then, clutching her elbow.

"Where should I sleep? I don't want to be an inconvenience," she said. Whenever she stayed the night, she crashed on the couch or floor. She almost expected that to remain true.

"Nonsense," he said and led the way down the hall. He kicked open the first door he came across. "This will be your room."

Claudia's eyes were a mixture of warmth and uncertainty as she looked around. It was much larger than the room she'd had at her parents' with a king size bed, dresser, flatscreen television, and walk-in closet. "Are you sure?"

"Positive," he said and tossed her bags onto the bed. Before she could protest, he unzipped her suitcase, pulling out a handful of her clothes. As the fabric scattered across the bed, it was hard to miss the frilly underwear among the rest. He couldn't resist running his hands through it all. Like in a way, he was claiming it and indirectly claiming her.

Claudia let out a nervous chuckle and hurried forward. "I can do that."

He didn't listen, only pausing when he came across something that *wasn't* clothing. A bundle of papers. He held it up with a smile. "Is this your book?"

Claudia clasped her hands together in front of her and gave a sheepish nod. In a way, it looked as if she were more embarrassed for him to see her book than her lingerie.

"It looks finished," he said, thumbing through the pages before he looked back up at her. "I thought you said you were still working on it."

"It is, but the agents I've shared it with have said there's a lack of believability in some of the murder scenes," Claudia said. "Honestly, I'm not sure how to look into reworking them without being put on some kind of FBI watch list."

"Hmm," he said, tapping the back of his fingers against the first page in thought. "Mind if I read it?"

She frowned and her bottom lip jutted out into a pout. It looked as if she were waiting for the perfect moment to pitch forward and snatch the papers out of his hand.

Just to be sure she wouldn't, he switched hands, eyeing her curiously. "What is it?"

"It's just…I'm afraid you'll laugh," she said.

A chuckle fell from León's lips. She had to be joking. "Why would I do that?"

"Well…I mean, this is your *life*. You *do* these kinds of things, and the most knowledge I have comes from television," she pointed out.

"See, now, I don't know if that's right or not because I haven't read it," he said, smiling wolfishly at her. "Only way for me to decide who wins this argument would be to see for myself."

Claudia hadn't been willing to waiver much in her decision. He'd gotten her to a point where she sounded uncertain but hadn't given him a definite answer. León waited until she fell asleep. He crept into her room, pausing beside her open bag on the floor. Her manuscript was still there, and he almost admired her innocence. If he was her, he would've hidden it. Scooping it up, he peered at her once again to make sure she was fully asleep before he went back to his own room.

He sat in bed, opening it up to the first page. He started to read and found he was unable to stop. The murders were elaborative, creative. After he read the first gory scene, he'd stared off into space before he found himself wandering into her room just to look at her. She was still sound asleep, wavy hair wild around her face and lips pressed into a soft pout. She'd changed into a soft camisole tank top and hadn't bothered to put any bottoms on over her matching underwear.

She could've been a model. Surely a girl of that caliber could *never* be depraved enough to write the things he'd read, and yet, she was. Shaking his head, he went back to his room and finished her book, awed by every page. Her writing made his dark fantasies look like sweet daydreams. He was so elated with the bloody scenes bounding through his head that he went into Claudia's room again and stared down at her.

He had the strangest urge to touch her, to run his hands over her every curve, and he wondered what she would do if he crawled in bed with her. He reached out, stroking her cheek to see what she would do. She made a slight groan in her throat, and he smiled, watching her turn onto her side. He spent another solid minute at her bedside before he bent down and pressed a kiss to her forehead.

Silently, he crept into the hallway, snagging his bag from its place under the couch. That night was the night he would become an official serial killer.

11.

CLAUDIA WAS WOKEN by the sun streaming through the window. The night before she hadn't realized she'd left the blinds open. Groaning, she rolled over and jolted upright when she realized she wasn't in her own bed. Then she remembered what had happened and relaxed.

Running her hand through her curls to get them into somewhat of an order, she threw on a T-shirt and some leggings before she got up and went to the bathroom. She didn't see León in the hall, but she wanted to make sure she was somewhat presentable just in case. For all she knew, he wasn't even home.

Yawning, she wandered into the living room and picked up the smell of coffee. Following it, she ended up in the kitchen. León was seated at the table wearing a white muscle shirt and baggy white and black checkered pajama pants. There was a piece of toast hanging from his mouth as he jotted something on the papers before him, leg bouncing in rhythm. She blinked and then her eyes stretched wide in recognition. That was her book.

At last, he must've felt her eyes on him because he looked up and pulled the toast from his mouth. "Good morning," he said, gray eyes flashing. "There's some coffee if you're interested."

"Morning," she replied and poured herself a cup. She eyed him for a moment before she moved back to the table and sat in the seat across from him. "You been up long?"

"Actually, I never went to bed," he said and tossed his pen down with a clang. Upon closer observation, she could see the dark half-circles under his eyes, but his smile made them harder to decipher.

"Ah," she said and took a sip of the coffee. The liquid was warm but not hot. She guessed he'd made it a few hours prior. "Is that my book?"

He nodded. "I hope you don't mind, but it is *fantastic*. I uh, made some notes if you're interested."

Claudia took the papers, reading through León's fancy script. There were additional pages filled with nothing but his writing, and she was touched that he'd done that for her. "These are helpful, thank you." Then she paused as one of the notes caught her eye, and she lowered them. "Wait. Have you ever…done someone in like this?"

León flashed her a proud little grin and popped the last of his toast in his mouth. "Before last night? No, but let's just say you've inspired me to pick up my A game."

Claudia gaped at him, a mix of emotions inside of her. Someone was dead because of her choice to be silent. Someone was dead, and it wasn't *her*. "You did it? Kill number three?" she asked in a hushed whisper.

He bobbed his head and swigged down the last bit of orange juice in his glass. "Yep. Using your idea. These notes, they are a detailed account of what happened."

Claudia pushed away her guilt. The depraved part of her brain was quick to remind her he'd done that for her. She smiled wide enough to show her teeth and hugged the papers to her chest. "You are the best! Thank you."

He smiled back, reaching under the table to clutch her knee.

"No. Thank *you*."

Exhausted, León went to sleep not long after that, and Claudia went to work checking her email and sending query letters to publishers. With León's additions, she was positive she had a solid manuscript. Confident that she had put in a solid day's work, she found herself pacing up and down the hallway. Once, she peeked into León's room to see if he'd woken up. He was wearing only his boxers, and Claudia immediately felt as if she were violating his privacy.

Ducking out of his room, she closed the door behind her and went back to pacing. Before she knew it, she was seated in front of her laptop again, pulling up her email. Usually, it took weeks, sometimes months for her to get a response, but an agent had already hit her back, requesting to read her entire manuscript.

Claudia was elated. She had never gotten so far into the query process before. As quickly as she could, she gathered up the materials and emailed them off.

12.

BY THE TIME León woke up, the sky was purple with twilight, and Claudia was gone. She'd left him a note saying she was at work and had good news she couldn't wait to share. He held the paper tight and smiled.

León was glad for her, and that struck him because he meant it. He was genuinely happy for another human being though not at glad as he was for himself. Last night had been like an invigorating trip to a spa. It had been a good while since he'd felt such satisfaction, and he reveled in the feeling.

Closing his eyes, flashes of his night came to him. Victim number three had not gone quickly. He'd drawn it out, pulling as much self-gratification as he could before disposing of her in a lake in Katy.

He didn't think of her again after that. Instead, he found himself wandering into Claudia's room just to get a hint of her scent. She'd left a pile of her old clothes on the floor, and he picked up the camisole she'd worn to sleep, bringing it close to his face to take a deep inhale. The sensations sweeping over him were strange. Of course he had known she was a woman, but it was as if he hadn't picked up on her femininity, her sexuality, until he'd read her book.

Shivering, he tossed the shirt back to the floor and forced himself to leave the room. He wasn't sure what it was that he wanted from Claudia anymore. He'd *never* really known, but her living with him meant he'd have to figure it out.

In the meantime, he craved a distraction. Head down, he snagged his keys and hurried out of the house with the decision to go down to the police station. It'd be worth seeing if they had any work for him. Plus, it wouldn't hurt to catch up with some old friends.

13.

CLAUDIA FOUND HER happiness made her a better dancer. Even though the last twenty-four hours had been rocky, she felt as if she'd taken strong steps to make her life better. Things were looking up for her career, and they were bound to improve with León too. That night, her tips were much higher than what she was used to, and when she looked up into the crowds, she was surprised to catch sight of León in the shadows.

The look on his face was *dangerous*. A cat stalking a mouse. The only time he'd ever looked at her like that was that first night, when he'd wrestled her into his truck. He was ready to spring and devour her whole. Claudia's mood dropped then. When he'd *had* the chance to do exactly that, he'd passed it up.

Claudia had a moment then where she wondered about her decision to move in with León. After all, she still had no idea what his true intentions were just as she didn't know what to expect since he'd committed another kill. She was glad her veil kept most of her expression hidden from the audience. Otherwise, they'd have noticed her frown.

When her time in the spotlight was done, she went to the backroom, carefully cleaning herself up. She took her time. Usually, knowing León was waiting for her filled her with sunshine, but the look he'd given her was still burned into her brain. Had she made a mistake accepting his offer? Did he think it meant they had to up their relationship?

When Claudia was out of ways to stall for time, she bit the bullet and went outside. León was leaning against the wall, waiting for her. He held his arm out, encouraging her to loop hers through it.

"The show was phenomenal tonight," he said as they walked across the parking lot.

Claudia blushed. Even though he'd come to her show before, that was the first time he'd really complimented her on it. "Thank you."

He opened her door for her, and she climbed inside, watching as León circled the truck to get into the driver seat. She fidgeted with the seatbelt, trying to ignore her sudden discomfort. After all they'd been through, it didn't make sense for her to feel that way then.

When she looked up, he was staring at her with that predatory expression on his face again. Before she could ask what it meant, he leaned across the center console and kissed her. Claudia didn't respond at first, and he reached his hand around the back of her head, grip tightening in a way that gave him better access to her. Heavy and frenzied, their mouths moved in sync until at last, Claudia pulled away, gasping for breath.

"León, I—"

"What is it?" he croaked, eyes and voice filled with lust. He didn't move his hand from the back of her neck, and she was caught staring up into his shadowy eyes as she struggled for words.

What did this mean? They'd known each other for almost two months, and the most he'd touched her was the first night when they'd fought one another getting into his truck. It wasn't a coincidence that this behavior had come after his crowning kill. They were related somehow, and Claudia was uneasy. A lot of serial killers linked sex and violence, but for some reason, she hadn't assumed León to be the kind. Or that he'd turn that energy to her.

Claudia wanted to push him away. It wasn't as if she were a virgin by any means, but she had the feeling that sex with León would be far different from any of the men she'd previously been with.

León's expression sharpened as if he could read every thought in her eyes. She still hadn't spoken. Hadn't explained why she'd disrupted the moment.

"I didn't even get to tell you my good news," she said, trying to downplay her hesitation and distract him at the same time.

León smiled and let go of her, situating himself back into his seat. He put the truck into reverse and backed out of their parking spot. As he shifted the gears, he said, "Tell me what it is now because when we get home, I'm hardly gonna give you time to breathe."

Claudia threaded her fingers together more nervous for what was to come than she had been at the idea of her own death. She looked down at her hands, trying to figure out why that was happening.

The book, she thought. He'd read her book and used her ideas. In his mind, it must have made him feel a closeness to her that had otherwise been absent.

"I have an agent interested in my book," she said at last.

"That's fantastic," he said.

"It's nothing confirmed yet," she continued, words coming out in a rapid tumble. "But she wanted to read the entire thing. If all goes well, she'll offer me a deal for representation and then shop the book around."

León smiled so wide that even in the darkness Claudia could see his teeth. "Well, it's a fantastic book. They'd be fools to not take you."

They were supportive words, but something about the way he said them didn't sit right with Claudia. They almost came across as a threat.

Her heart started to pound a little faster as León's neighborhood came into view, and as he pulled the truck to a halt in his driveway, she felt herself stiffen. The truck was barely idle before he lunged at her, unbuckling her seat belt as he kissed her like a deprived man. She didn't struggle, and he pulled her right against his body, pulling back a minute later.

"Come on," he said, voice thick with lust again.

He was the first one out of the truck, and Claudia a moment behind. As soon as she came to his side, he grabbed her again, pressing himself against her. When she'd peeked into his room, she'd caught sight of how sculpted he was, but then, she could really tell just how much muscle tone he had. It was like a dance as he moved her across the lawn and through the front door kissing her and running his hands along her curves the entire way.

Claudia tried to break herself free, but León didn't let her go until they were in his room. His hands were anything but gentle, grabbing and squeezing her hips, butt, and anything else. He pushed her onto the bed with such force the breath was knocked from her lungs.

Winded, she stared up at him. León discarded his shirt and smiled down at her before he knelt on the edge of the bed, stripping her out of every piece of fabric on her body. Tongue trailing her jawbone, his fingers explored her skin. When he pulled back to strip off the rest of his clothes, Claudia self-consciously pulled his white sheet up over her body.

Just when she thought he'd climb into the bed, he turned to the tiny nightstand beside him. He opened the drawer and pulled out a butcher knife. Claudia sat straight up, trying to back away from him. The time when she'd been ready to die seemed like such a long time ago.

He stared down at her with an impossible to decipher expression, the blade catching in the moonlight streaming through his blinds. She didn't have to touch it to know it was sharp. Before she could ask, he pounced. One hand went to her throat, holding her slack against the bed. With the hand holding the knife, he grabbed the sheet and thrust it aside, exposing her body.

With a smile, he turned the blade toward her. She opened her mouth to cry out, but he was too quick. With a slash, he opened a line between her ribs. She gasped in pain, that turned to shock when his mouth settled over the wound, tongue lapping up her blood in slow seductive strokes.

"Wh…" she wheezed.

Blackness started to encroach on the edges of her vision when he made the second slash. Three more slashes followed, and the blackness took over her vision as she faded out of consciousness.

When Claudia came back to reality, it took her a moment to remember what had happened. She and León were tangled in his white sheets, splotches of her blood soaking it through in some places. Claudia didn't look at it, not wanting to remember how it had gotten there. She stared up at the ceiling, body aching in a mix of pain and pleasure. She was surprised to still be alive, confident that León had been ready to kill her. From the corner of her eye, she could see him watching her, face warped in rapt fascination.

"You did so well," he said, softly running his finger down her forearm. "All that dancing really does wonders for your endurance."

Claudia shivered, cold with vulnerability. She wanted to go back into the blackness where he could not follow.

"Are you okay?" he asked, frowning as he realized she still hadn't spoken.

"I…I'm fine," she said at last.

"Then look at me."

Claudia forced her head to turn in his direction. She stared at his lips, finding it hard to look into his eyes.

"Did I scare you?" he asked, ducking his face to catch her eye anyway.

Claudia pursed her lips and turned onto her side, facing away from him. It was impossible for her to describe exactly what emotions were going through her. None of them were positive.

"I realize what I do is a bit unorthodox," he said. "That's why it's been a while since I've really let myself get close to anyone. I've found my…*kinks*…are a bit much for the ordinary woman to handle."

Claudia blinked. The comment stung, but her body hurt more.

He sighed. "Well, I'd say talk to me when you feel like it, but I'm not going to be here for a while."

Claudia frowned and peered at him over her shoulder. "Where are you going?"

"I have a new bounty to track down. Some idiot hijacked an armored truck and fled the state."

"That sounds dangerous."

"It is what it is," León conceded. "Are you going to be okay with me gone?"

After this, of course, Claudia thought. Out loud she said, "I'll make do."

14.

WHEN CLAUDIA WOKE up, León was already gone. She sat up, pressing the white sheet to her chest and winced. The spots of blood had dried to a hard crusty grime that scratched her skin every place they touched. Claudia barely paid it much attention as she looked side to side, trying to determine if León was still somewhere around. Part of her was certain he was lying in wait, ready to catch her off guard.

Positive she was alone, she looked down at herself. The cuts he'd left along her ribs and upper torso were ugly, a deep angry red that bled into the skin around them. Mixed into the haze of cuts was a particularly nasty bite mark and dozens of purple-black bruises. She looked as if she'd been in a fight rather than what they had actually done.

She hadn't expected León to be gentle, but he had somehow surpassed her expectations. Shivering with the desire to be clean, she wrapped the sheet around herself and crossed the hall to the bathroom. Usually, she wasn't a fan of hot showers because they left her skin feeling too dry, but that morning, she used only the hot water. Her skin felt as if it were burning when she finally stepped out. Without the dried blood crusted to her though, the wounds didn't look as bad as she'd initially guessed them to be.

Even still, as she got dressed, she was glad she wouldn't have to look at León for a while. It was still hard for her to wrap her brain around the drastic change their friendship had taken.

To distract herself, she opened her laptop, going to her email. The agent had sent a response.

Claudia,

Just finished the book. I absolutely love it. Please give me a call at the following number so we can talk business.

Claudia was elated. So elated that all her negative feelings disappeared. She reached for her phone, expecting to see a message from León, but there was nothing. She supposed that he'd told her all he was going to about his location the night before.

That was fine with her. Before Claudia dialed the agent's number, she thumbed through her call logs, ignoring all the ones from her mother. In that moment, she wished she could call her and tell her the good news. That she could tell *someone.* Ever since she'd moved out, Claudia had gone out of her way to ignore her parents. Not that she was mad at them. She wasn't. It was more along the lines of the fact that it made her easier for her to cling to her decision that way.

A clean break.

They say those always heal the quickest, the easiest, and yet, Claudia wasn't sure. She'd answered the phone to her mother only once since she moved in with León, just to ensure her parents that she was still alive. She thought of León's change again and her mother's words *I'm worried about his intentions.*

Maybe it would've been better off to let them think she *was* dead.

15.

TWO MONTHS PASSED. Claudia went about her life as if nothing had changed. Really, the only thing that had was her agent and Leon's disappearance. She *had* an agent then, and a book that was queued to be published. Think what she wanted about León, but he was at least partly responsible for her success.

As time passed, she found herself missing him more and more. The nights they'd spent together before his crowning kill had been some of the best of her life. Even though things had taken a turn, she hoped they could still go back to that. She supposed that hope was what kept her at León's even though the advance she'd received from the publisher was more than enough for her to get her own place.

Claudia only left León's to go to work, unsure when he'd return. When he had told her he'd be leaving, she'd assumed for a few days. A week at most. She started to wonder if he planned on coming back. He hadn't left a way to contact him, and at first, Claudia hadn't minded that fact. For a while, she hadn't *wanted* to contact him, but then, it bothered her.

Claudia put most of her frustrations into her dances. Even when she was home alone, she distracted herself by stretching and trying out new moves. She was physically exhausted often, but having a goal was good. It took her mind off things and made the time go by faster.

One night, when she'd danced to the point of collapse, she sat down and turned on the TV, waiting to cool down. Her heart raced, and she feared it would give out. A result of too many energy drinks as a teenager.

"In local news today, the hunt for missing girl, Laura

Andrews, has come to a tragic end. Her remains were found in a drainage ditch just outside of Houston. Police haven't released details on the case, but it is believed Miss Andrews if the third victim of the Houston Butcher."

The TV changed to a smiling image of the girl. Claudia stared at her, clutching the remote tightly. Something ached inside her. Laura looked like León's other two girls which were to say nothing like Claudia herself. Claudia let the remote fall to the floor and folded her hands in her lap, unsure how to feel. At the very least, she knew why she was still alive, and they weren't.

16.

LEON WAS COMPLETELY exhausted as he led the man in handcuffs into the police station. Two months of chasing him down. Two months of sleeping in his truck and binging on nothing but fast food, and all he could think about was Claudia. He'd thought about her nonstop from the moment he'd walked out the front door. Leaving the bed with her delicate body wrapped in his sheets was one of the hardest things he'd ever had to do.

In an effort to stay distant, he'd left her no way to check up on him, but he hadn't done the same. Every day, he checked her social media. He'd been over the moon to see the news about her book, and then a bit disappointed that he wasn't there with her to celebrate. That only left him wondering once again if she missed him. The last time he'd seen her, she hadn't even wanted to look at him. The absent look she'd given him made him frown briefly. Whatever she had felt, he could fix by being there for her big day. On the hunt, all he could do was watch launch day come closer and closer. He started to think he'd miss it when his target finally slipped up, and León was rewarded for his patience.

And not a moment too soon. Tomorrow was the day.

He stifled a yawn as he led the man to booking and collected his check. Yearning to see Claudia again, he hurried out into the cool night air and drove home. Outside his house, he could hear Claudia long before he saw her. As he stuck the key in the lock, the pulsing sound of music filled his ears. Inside, it was much louder. He followed the pattering sound of her feet to her room and peered inside, watching her twirl and bow.

She was so enraptured in her dance that she hadn't noticed him. Folding his arms over his chest, León leaned against the doorframe and studied her. She was thinner than he remembered, but other than that, everything looked to be the same. When her dance began to slow, he clapped.

Holding a hand to her chest, she whisked on her heels to stare at him, wide-eyed. Then her face cracked into an enormous smile. Nothing like the expression in his mind's eye. "You're back!"

She rushed toward him, wrapping her arms around his midsection. The smell of her skin aroused him, and just like then, he kissed her with that same animal passion. She didn't stop him.

An hour later, they were both spent. He hadn't gone as rough as he had the first time, but she still looked at him as if she weren't sure how to be around him in the aftermath.

He slung his arms out, bringing her close. "Are you uncomfortable with me?"

Slowly, she shook her head. "When we met, I just…never thought we'd end up like this."

León told himself not to be angry. It wasn't the way to handle this, to handle *her*, but he was still stung by the comment. "Do you still wish I'd killed you instead?"

"Yes and no," she admitted, threading his sheet through her fingers. "But I know why you didn't. I don't…look like the girls you pick. Your other victims. They're blond and pretty. Such fair skin. I know serial killers usually have a type and…I don't…meet yours."

He laughed and reached out to twirl a lock of her dark hair around his fingers. "You're pretty too. Wonderful complexion and healthy body. Superior to those others because not only are you beautiful to look at, you actually have a brain in your head."

"I don't look like Laura though," she murmured, not looking at him.

León stiffened. That was a name she shouldn't know. Hell, it was a name he barely knew except for the passing glance he'd given to the girl's driver's license while disposing of the evidence. Drawing his eyebrows together he said, "Laura?"

"Yeah. Your crowning kill?" she asked, peering up at him through her lashes.

"I know who she is. I'm just wondering how *you* know her name," he said, getting more and more aggravated for each moment that passed of this uncertain limbo.

"It was on the news. They found her," Claudia said. "They tied it to the other two girls."

"Damn," he murmured, reaching up to ruffle his hair. He had known he hadn't hidden her well, but he thought he'd at least have another month or two before anyone made the discovery. Claudia gave him a sympathetic look, face pinched as if she were almost afraid to have been the one to tell him. He didn't like the look and did what he could to quell his anger. "Don't worry about it, okay? Tomorrow is your day. I'll see what the police know about her case as soon as I can. Until then? No more talk."

He pressed his lips to hers, bringing her close to him once more.

17.

"**T**HANKS, EVERYONE," CLAUDIA said at the end of her speech.

The little crowd that had gathered in the tiny event room of the bookstore clapped and called their congratulations. As they got up to shuffle out of their seats, Claudia looked to León. He was leaning against the wall, just enough to be out of focus of the crowd while still getting the best vantage point of her reading. When they made eye contact, he beamed at her, the slightest hint of a smile on his face.

In all the time she'd known him, he hadn't looked so exuberant. Partly, she wondered what it was that made him look like that then. Was it her? Was it what they had done together? Or was it simply because he loved the darkness in her brain that much? Claudia was almost afraid to ask. Whatever the case, she was glad he was there, glad for his support.

At last he came up to her, pressing a kiss to her lips before he pulled her in for a hug. "I'm so proud of you," he whispered into her ear, fingers drawing lazy circles in her back.

She pulled away and looked up at him, wide-eyed. "You mean it?"

He chuckled and brushed a lock of hair from her face. "Of course. You are capable of so much more than you give yourself credit for."

"Claudia, sweetheart," a familiar voice said, and Claudia tensed, instantly alarmed.

"There you are!"

Before she knew it, she was being pulled away from León. She blinked and was left looking into the concerned faces of her parents. The expressions they wore were ones she was used to seeing. They looked at her as if she were a child, a little thing who had no idea what she was doing.

"It's been months, and you don't call. Don't even drop a message to let us know you're all right," Claudia's mom said, taking her face in her hands. "I've been so worried, *dragă*!"

"To see you've been messing around with this stuff. The therapist told you it was no good for you," her father said, waving a hand around the room. He wasn't having any of the sentiment. It was just like him.

León's eyes volleyed from one parent to the other. He could see from Claudia's stance that she was uncomfortable. "Hi there, you must be Claudia's parents," he said, something of a smile on his face as he interjected himself into the conversation.

"And who are you?" Claudia's mom asked, eyes looking him up and down as if he did nothing but disgust her.

Claudia held her breath, unsure what to say. She wasn't even sure what they were, but whatever it was, it was much too intense to be called friendship. Even before León spoke, she knew her parents wouldn't approve. He was, after all, the reason she'd moved out to begin with.

"Apologies," León said, giving a slight bow. "My name is León, and I must say you have a wonderful daughter."

"You are the reason my daughter no longer talks to me," the woman said, waving her finger at León. "I told her you were bad news, and she didn't want to listen."

"Stop it, Momma," Claudia said, watching the corner of León's lip twitch, flickering between a smile and a snarl. "I love you, but you're suffocating me. León lets me breathe, lets me explore the places in my head that you won't."

"You are a bad influence on my daughter," Claudia's father reiterated. He grabbed a copy of Claudia's book from the nearby table and waved it in León's face. "She is fragile. Too fragile for this."

León looked at Claudia with a purposeful raise of his eyebrows.

"I respectfully disagree, sir. I think I bring out the best in her." He snatched the book from Claudia's father and kissed the cover.

"You smug little—" her father roared and lunged at him.

"Daddy! No!" Claudia said and stepped between them. "Please, stop fighting."

"You're coming home with us now," Claudia's mother said, grabbing the top of Claudia's arm so hard that her nails made the skin an angry color.

"She's not going anywhere," León retorted, grabbing her other arm.

Tears of humiliation swam in her eyes. León and her parents were literally playing tug-o-war with her at that point, and everyone was watching. "Stop it!" Claudia said again. She dug her knuckles into her temples before she said, "I'm a grown woman."

"That's why you should come with me," León said, chin raised as his gaze went again from her mother to her father. "No one can vouch for your womanhood more than me."

"Are you having sex with this man?" her mother asked, face alight with horror.

Claudia felt the color drain from her face. She wanted to speak in her defense but felt as if her tongue were suddenly too large for her mouth.

"Of course she is," León said, cocky expression on his face. "Your daughter is mine now."

Her father opened his mouth to yell again, but Claudia didn't wait. She ripped herself free from León and her mother and said, "That's enough!"

León's smugness faded as he turned to look at her.

Tears dripped down her face as she said, "P-please just give me some space. Let me talk to my parents."

Something flitted across his eyes. Something she couldn't register. Something *dangerous*. "Fine. I'll give you all the *space* you can handle," he said and tossed the copy of her book at her before he shouldered his way past Claudia's dad on the way out the door.

18.

LEON BARELY MADE it to his truck before he screamed at the top of his lungs. In the driver's seat, he punched the steering wheel over and over, wondering how much it would take before it ejected the air bag and punched him back.

How could Claudia not have his back? After everything they'd been through together, how could she doubt him for even a minute? He stayed in the truck, looking into the sideview mirror to keep an eye on the front door. Claudia or her parents didn't appear, so he put the key in the engine.

A nice drive might help contain his rage. Before he knew it, he was at the police station. He stared up at the side of the building, thinking just how ironic his entire existence was. He was a murderer, yet he hunted down criminals. He had helped Claudia build her life back up, and then, she pushed him away.

Angry again, he climbed out of the truck and went inside. There had to be another case he could work. Something that would take him away from home for a few days until the dust settled. He sat at the table, thumbing through the bounty cases on file.

"I'm sure it's just a coincidence," a voice said from down the hall.

"Awfully funny that the method of death matches sentence for sentence."

"Houston is a big city, lot of books have been written about this place."

León swallowed but didn't move. It sounded an awful lot like they were talking about Claudia's book. *You're being paranoid,* he told himself, but as he bent over the binder, he was no longer reading the words before him. His ears were perked, drinking in every word from the hall.

"The timing is too much for my liking," the first man continued.

"The book just came out today. You don't think this Claudia girl could've done it, tested out her own ideas?"

"That'd be kind of stupid, wouldn't it?"

"Didn't say it wasn't, but it's a place to start."

León no longer cared about the anger in the pit of his stomach. He waited until the officers were gone before he moved as fast as he could. He kept his head down, sure his fear was written across his face. They suspected Claudia which meant they would make their way to him. That was the day he'd dreaded for some time. He needed to split town before it was too late.

León hopped into his truck, running through his plan. He had an emergency bag ready under his bed. All he'd have to do was grab it and go. Part of him ached at the thought of leaving Claudia. He couldn't understand it. The entire drive home, he told himself over and over again that it didn't matter. He would be just fine without her, wherever he ended up. Hadn't she pretty much told him to leave anyway?

So why do I feel like this?

When he pulled into his driveway, he expected to go into an empty house. Surely after what had happened, Claudia would've gone home with her parents and forgotten all about him.

She was seated on the couch. When he entered, she stood up instantly. "Oh, God. There you are. I'm so sorry about my parents."

"Don't be. They can have you back," he said, hurrying down the hallway to his room.

"Wait, what?" she asked.

The patter of soft footsteps on the floorboards told him

she was close behind. He glanced over his shoulder to see how close as he rounded the frame to go into his room. He bent down on his hands and knees, seeking out his bag. He grabbed it just as he felt Claudia's hand on his shoulder.

"León, stop. Please. What's going on?" she asked, voice soft and fragile.

Sighing, he turned to look at her. Her eyes looked huge with worry, fear, and uncertainty. The expression tugged at something in him, but he pushed it away, telling himself it was for the best if he severed the ties between them. If there was no relationship, the cops couldn't tie him to her.

"I'm leaving, alright? It's over. Whatever this is," he said at last and stood up, slinging his bag over his shoulder. He tried to step past her when she stepped into his path, blocking him.

"Is this because of what happened today?" she demanded.

Flaring his nostrils, he looked down his nose at her. "No, but they're part of it, definitely."

"What's the rest?" she asked, once again blocking him from taking a step farther out of the room.

He reached up, running his finger along his lip before he said, "Someone gave a tip to the police about your book." She blinked uncertainly, so he added. "They compared your scene to Laura. They know."

"They know it was you?" she asked, eyes wide again.

León hated the concern he could see on her face. She was actually *worried* about him. Not herself. *No one's ever looked at me like that,* he thought. "No, but they know it's connected. I don't know if they know about *us,* but they want to question you. If they do, they'll realize it's me. That I'm the Butcher."

"So you're leaving?" she asked, eyes moving to his bag as if it was the first time she was actually seeing it.

He bobbed his head. "I'm leaving. It's the only way to get out of this."

Claudia reached out to grab his arm, eyes hardening into dark pieces of flint. "You can't just leave me behind. Not after everything we've been through."

León scoffed and tried to pull his arm free. "You're the one who wanted space, right?"

"Not like this," she said, digging her nails into his wrist so that her grip couldn't be dislodged regardless of how he pulled. "I want to go with you."

"Why would you do that?" he asked, confused for the gesture but at the same time not wanting her to know just how confused he really was. "You can tell them it was me, and your life will continue as it was before I ever entered it. No harm, no foul."

"You might not get this, but it's possible to bond with people without killing them. Remember? That's why you *didn't* kill me. Think of all the nights we've spent together. We go well together, León. Please, don't end things like this."

León didn't know what to think. Her eyes were so honest; he could swear that looking into their depths he could see her very soul. He'd heard of friendship, of love, but had never experienced either. Until then. Leaving Claudia behind was something he didn't want to do. And not just because she was the only one who knew the truth of whom and what he was.

He couldn't imagine his life without her in it—without the sound of her dancing, and the scent of her perfume. She had gotten under his skin, and no matter how long he lived, he would always desire her.

He gave in. "Okay. Hurry up and pack."

Claudia raced down the hall, and León found that he was

smiling as he followed after her. She took no time at all to pack and slung her bag over her shoulders, face calm and ready. When he met her eyes, she smiled at him. León smiled back, feeling real warmth for possibly the first time in his life. He held his hand out, and Claudia took it. Where they'd go from there, he wasn't sure. With Claudia by his side though, he was sure they'd be just fine.

About the Author

Kayla Frederick is the new pen name for established author, Kayla Krantz. A little neurotic and a huge lover of Halloween, she enjoys creepy stories.

9 781950 530250